The 12 DAYS of CHRISTMAS

By Linnea Asplind Riley

Simon & Schuster Books for Young Readers

Acknowledgments

Musical arrangement of "The Twelve Days of Christmas"
by Adam Stemple, from *HARK! A Christmas Sampler* by Jane Yolen,
reprinted by permission of G. P. Putnam's Sons and by permission
of Curtis Brown, Ltd. Musical arrangement copyright © 1991
by Adam Stemple.

SIMON & SCHUSTER BOOKS FOR YOUNG READERS
An imprint of Simon & Schuster Children's Publishing Division
1230 Avenue of the Americas, New York, New York 10020
Copyright © 1995 by Linnea Asplind Riley
Simon & Schuster Books for Young Readers
is a trademark of Simon & Schuster.
Book design by Paul Zakris
The text for this book is set in 31-point Albertus.
The illustrations are made of cut and painted paper.
Manufactured in Singapore
10 9 8 7 6 5 4 3 2 1

Library of Congress Catalog Card Number: 95-76077
ISBN 0-689-80275-7

Illustrator's Note

"The Twelve Days of Christmas" song began long ago in medieval times in France or England, nobody knows for sure. It was a kind of party game set to music and was written especially for singing on Twelfth-Night, the eve of Epiphany. The first person sang a stanza and the second player sang his own addition plus the original lines. The game continued with the last player having the most difficult time remembering all the twelve gifts and their order.

The discovery of many centuries-old manuscripts of the song reveal the constant change and personalization of the song's vocabulary as it was tailored to fit various regions. In fact, the first gift of the song may have been the result of a barely bilingual individual's misunderstanding of the old French words for partridge: "Une pertriz," which is pronounced something akin to "in a pear tree" (Martha Bennett Stiles, "A Partridge in an Etymologicon: The Truth about that Pear Tree," *Stereo Review* 35, no. 6, December 1975). The "four calling birds" are surely an auditory confusion of "four colly birds." Colly or collied means soot-blackened or coal black, most probably black birds. The gold rings were probably another garbling. Being as the first four gifts and the sixth and seventh ones are birds, number five may have been either ring-necked pheasants or gulderers (turkeys) (Douglas Brice, *The Folk-Carol of England*, London: Herbert Jenkins Ltd., 1967).

Regardless of the choice of words or their order of appearance, the fact that "The Twelve Days of Christmas" is still with us after so many centuries proves its belovedness. Here is another opportunity to find and count all the true love's gifts to his lady.

For Michael

n the first day of Christmas
my true love gave to me...

a partridge in a pear tree.

On the second day of Christmas
my true love gave to me

2 turtle doves

and a partridge in a pear tree.

On the third day of Christmas
my true love gave to me
3 French hens,

2 *turtle doves,*

and a partridge in a pear tree.

On the fourth day of Christmas
my true love gave to me
4 colly birds,

3 French hens,

2 turtle doves,

and a partridge in a pear tree.

On the fifth day of Christmas
my true love gave to me
5 gold rings,

4 colly birds,
3 French hens,
2 turtle doves,
and a partridge in a pear tree.

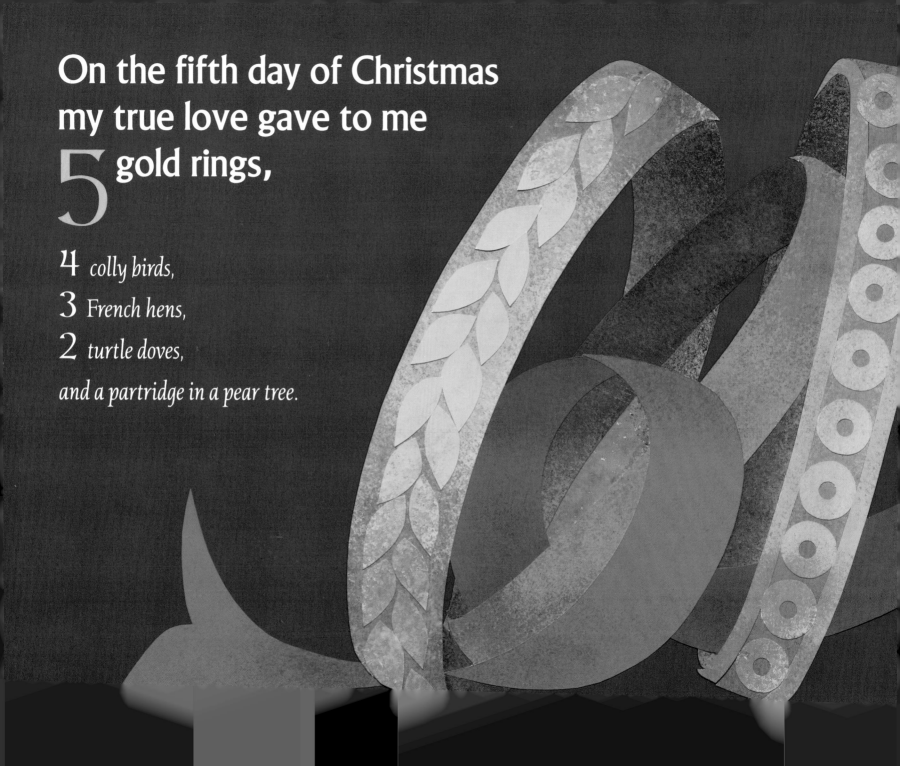

On the sixth day of Christmas
my true love gave to me
6 geese a-laying,

5 gold rings,
4 colly birds,
3 French hens,
2 turtle doves,
and a partridge in a pear tree.

On the seventh day of Christmas
my true love gave to me

7 swans a-swimming,

6 *geese a-laying,*
5 *gold rings,*
4 *colly birds,*
3 *French hens,*
2 *turtle doves,*
and a partridge in a pear tree.

On the eighth day of Christmas
my true love gave to me
8 maids a-milking,

7 swans a-swimming,

6 geese a-laying,

5 gold rings,

4 colly birds,

3 French hens,

2 turtle doves,

and a partridge in a pear tree.

On the ninth day of Christmas
my true love gave to me
9 ladies dancing,

8 maids a-milking,

7 swans a-swimming,

6 geese a-laying,

5 gold rings,

4 colly birds,

3 French hens,

2 turtle doves,

and a partridge in a pear tree.

On the tenth day of Christmas
my true love gave to me

10 lords a-leaping,

9 ladies dancing,

8 maids a-milking,

7 swans a-swimming,

6 geese a-laying,

5 gold rings,

4 colly birds,

3 French hens,

2 turtle doves,

and a partridge in a pear tree.

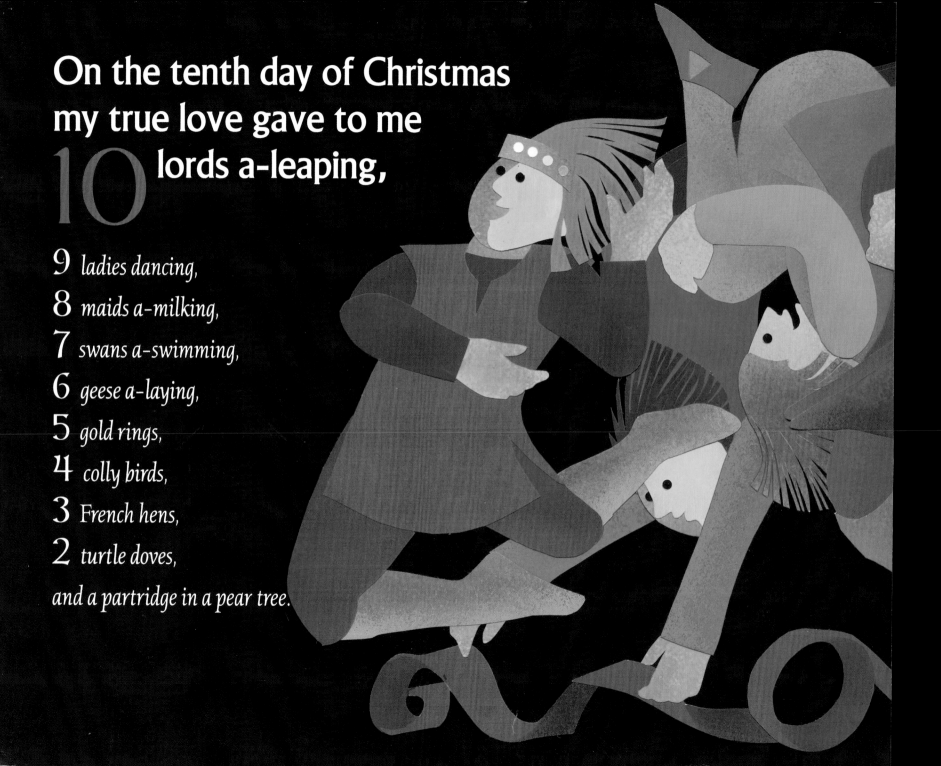

On the eleventh day of Christmas my true love gave to me

11 pipers piping,

10 lords a-leaping,
9 ladies dancing,
8 maids a-milking,
7 swans a-swimming,
6 geese a-laying,
5 gold rings,
4 colly birds,
3 French hens,
2 turtle doves,
and a partridge in a pear tree.

On the twelfth day of Christmas
my true love gave to me

12 drummers drumming,

11 pipers piping,
10 lords a-leaping,
9 ladies dancing,
8 maids a-milking,
7 swans a-swimming,
6 geese a-laying,
5 gold rings,
4 colly birds,
3 French hens,
2 turtle doves,
and a partridge in a pear tree.

true love gave to me Five gold— rings, Four— col - ly birds,

Three French hens, Two— tur - tle doves And a par - tridge in a pear tree.

accumulative

D.S. al Fine

sixth
seventh
eighth
On the ninth day of Christ - mas, My true love gave to me
tenth
eleventh
twelfth

Six geese a - lay - ing,
Seven swans a - swim - ming,
Eight maids a - milk - ing,
Nine la - dies danc - ing,
Ten lords a - leap - ing,
Eleven pip - ers pip - ing,
Twelve drum - mers drum - ming,

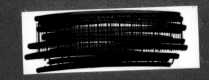